All children have a great ambition to read to themselves...and a sense of achievement when they can do so.

The **read it yourself** *series has been devised to satisfy their ambition. Even before children begin to learn to read formally, perhaps using a reading scheme, it is important that they have books and stories which will actively encourage the development of essential pre-reading skills. Books at Level 1 in this series have been devised with this in mind and will supplement pre-reading books available in any reading scheme.*

Children need to develop left to right eye movements and to perceive differences in word and letter shapes. Based on well-known nursery rhymes and games which children will have heard, these simple pre-readers introduce key words and phrases which children will meet in later reading. These are repeated and the full-colour artwork provides picture clues for new words.

Many young children will remember the words rather than read them but this is a normal part of pre-reading. It is recommended that the parent or teacher should read the book aloud to the child first and then go through the story, with the child reading the text.

British Library Cataloguing in Publication Data

Murdock, Hy
   What time is it Mr. Wolf?.—(Read it yourself. Level 1).
   1. Readers—1950-
   I. Title   II. Breeze, Lynn   III. Series
   428.6   PE1119

   ISBN 0-7214-0871-0

Published by Ladybird Books Ltd Loughborough Leicestershire UK
Ladybird Books Inc Auburn Maine 04210 USA

Printed in England

What time is it, Mr Wolf?

devised by Hy Murdock
illustrated by Lynn Breeze

Ladybird Books

What time is it, Mr Wolf?

It's six o'clock.

6 o'clock

I'm just awake.

What time is it, Mr Wolf?

It's half-past six.

half-past 6

I get out of bed.

What time is it, Mr Wolf?

7 o'clock

I'm washed and dressed.

What time is it, Mr Wolf?

It's eight o'clock.

8 o'clock

I eat my breakfast.

What time is it, Mr Wolf?

It's half-past eight.

half-past 8

I'm going to school.

What time is it, Mr Wolf?

It's nine o'clock.

9 o'clock

I like my teacher.

What time is it, Mr Wolf?

It's ten o'clock.

10 o'clock

I paint a picture.

What time is it, Mr Wolf?

half-past 10

I write a story.

What time is it, Mr Wolf?

11 o'clock

I'm making some cakes.

What time is it, Mr Wolf?

It's twelve o'clock.

12 o'clock

I eat my sandwiches.

What time is it, Mr Wolf?

It's one o'clock.

1 o'clock

I play with my friends.

What time is it, Mr Wolf?

2 o'clock

I jump on the mat.

What time is it, Mr Wolf?

It's three o'clock.

3 o'clock

I like to sing.

What time is it, Mr Wolf?

half-past 3

I put on my coat.

What time is it, Mr Wolf?

It's four o'clock.

4 o'clock

I'm home again.

What time is it, Mr Wolf?

It's five o'clock.

5 o'clock

I'm watching television.

What time is it, Mr Wolf?

It's six o'clock.

6 o'clock

I'm eating my dinner.

What time is it, Mr Wolf?

It's half-past seven.

half-past 7

It's time for a story.

41